More Praise for *Oh My Darling*

What wondrous and magical stories Cate O'Toole has woven in these dark, revisionist tales of Clementine, who comes powerfully and heartbreakingly alive under O'Toole's ministrations. The brilliant format allows readers to choose how they move through the collection, and which narratives they want to privilege. Reminiscent of Angela Carter's *The Bloody Chamber*, O'Toole creates such utterly genuine and believable (if sometimes scary!) characters and landscapes you'll forget you are reading fiction. And you'll never listen to "Oh, My Darling, Clementine" in the same way after reading this book.
—Sheryl St. Germain, author of *Navigating Disaster: Sixteen Essays of Love and a Poem of Despair*

In *Oh My Darling*, Cate O'Toole invites us to take part in the highs and lows of the California gold rush. Each decision we make as Clementine, a miner's daughter, brings us closer to love and fortune, or, just as easily, death and despair. With masterful, sometimes unflinching, prose, O'Toole paints the harsh realities of the untamed West where mere survival is a challenge. She asks us again and again what it is we really want, what it is we really need, and as we navigate Clementine's many possible lives, we must decide what we're really after: gold, love, or something closer to contentment.
—Rebecca King, Origami Zoo Press

CATE O'TOOLE

OH MY DARLING

Black
Lawrence
Press

Black
Lawrence
Press

www.blacklawrence.com

Executive Editor: Diane Goettel
Chapbook Editor: Kit Frick
Book and cover design: Amy Freels

Published 2015 by Black Lawrence Press.
Printed in the United States.

To the incredible broads of my workshop group,
for your support, your insight, your bottles of wine.

Clementine

At the last dusty town in a line of dusty towns, her father stops for supplies. Clementine unfolds from the back of the creaking wagon and follows him into the general store. Pa says, *Don't touch anything.*

When his back is turned, Clementine strokes a bolt of blue muslin, stains it with her fingers. Disgusted, she rubs her arms, dirt and skin flaking away like fish scales. She shakes the dust out of her skirts, spits on the worn floor. They've been traveling more than a month, filth their constant companion. Clementine wants a bath, a bed, an end to her journey. Heavy red dust and a deep, desperate yearning fill her days.

Pa, arms full of tools shining sharp and savage, comes on her picking apart knots in her long blonde hair. He frowns. He says, loud enough for everyone—miners and farmers, women with baskets and babies—to hear, *Clem, honey. You wait outside.*

She drags her feet over the threshold, cheeks burning. Fifteen and still being scolded—as though her father set any kind of example for decorum, weeping day and night for his dead wife and lost babies and sick, scabby farm. Such a small man, she thinks. Weakhearted. Clementine was glad to leave the farm, to leave her mother behind with her brothers and sisters. She didn't trouble to grieve at the time and she won't spare grief now.

Clementine watches a man with a black mustache roll a cigarette, finish with a twist. He leans against the porch rail as though he has never known trouble or hurry or gone without. His clothes are neat, only the barest crust of dirt on the hem of his pants, clinging to the heels of his boots. He catches her staring and tips his hat. He has thin lips, a round chin. His eyes dance a slow circuit over her. She feels his gaze on her hips, her breasts, her mouth. The man with the black mustache doesn't speak, but he is asking a question that Clementine knows she must answer.

Pa, coming out of the store, says, *Clem, honey?*

Something inside her, the heavy pit of badness she has carried west, begins to sing.

The Man with the Black Mustache—turn to p. 3
The Gold Claim—turn to p. 25

The Man with the Black Mustache

In his room at the boarding house, the man with the black mustache says, *We ought get married, Clementine,* and she agrees. He kisses her, and later she touches the spot over her lip where his mustache rasped her skin. The man sees and smiles. He says, *Cupid's bow.*

The man bathes her. Sends her dress to be washed and pressed. Loves her. One afternoon he borrows a wagon and drives to a hard, bare scrap of meadow, announces his intention to build them a home. *Soon,* the man says, flexing his hands. *Soon enough!* He is eager to start, swollen with plans. Clementine thinks of her father, stooped and small. She likes the idea of being a prosperous man's wife, living in a town and raising his happy children. No mining, no farm, no want or toil. Yes, she has been fortunate. Yes, she has struck a vein more precious than gold.

In the evening, the man excuses himself to the saloon and sits for hours with other men, laughing and growling and gnashing his teeth. Clementine lies in the man's narrow bed and prays for good luck and good hands. When his boots tread heavy down the hall, she sits up to greet him, arranges her hair in a yellow cascade over one shoulder.

The man with the black mustache fills up the doorway, casts shade on the bed. Clementine starts to say something wifely and the flat of his hand catches her ear. Such strong hands.

Endure—turn to p. 5
Escape—turn to p. 15

Endure

Bruises are no less than she deserves. Hasn't Clementine always had a streak in her, a devil on her shoulder? Her husband with the black mustache says his luck changed when she sauntered up to him, that he traded gold in his hand for the gold of her hair without knowing the terms of the bargain. He wages a great battle against fate with his fists, night after night.

Clementine tracks the progression of his anger on her skin—here a dusty, sprouted green, there purple as distant mountains—and in her split lips, her loosened teeth. She is conscious of crunching bone and rending hair even as she moves outside herself to watch the man beat her. She waits for some sign that the devil has been cast off, her husband's anger sated, but it will not be shaken. Its grip is deep as skin and blood and bone.

She thinks of her mother, hard-lined and grim, a broad woman crushed under the weight of despair. She thinks of influenza, her brothers and sisters in their cedar coffins. She thinks of those sweet dead children and understands at last the misfortune of survival. When she succumbs to the slack embrace of black night she sees their faces in her dreams. On waking she will turn her body again to her husband and hope to join them. He can give her that much.

But then there are some nights when the devil breathes fire within her, when a spark of fury zips down her spine. There are nights when her muscles burn with the urge to strike at her husband, to smother him as he sleeps, to stand at the door and watch the bedclothes burn. Even as Clementine comforts herself with the dream of death, her blood roars its own demand.

Fall—turn to p. 7
Fight—turn to p. 9

Fall

The man's fists sing on her skin, drowning out the devil's rumbling. Lovely music, sweet and melodious, though lacking a certain polish, finesse. Clementine allows her thoughts to wander, to find comfort in nonsense. *I am a harp*, she thinks, *and my back is strong and unyielding and my insides have disappeared, I am all strings and emptiness, waiting to be plucked. I am a drum, solid, held tight, and the world bounces off my skin and nothing can hurt me.*

Clementine sees shapes and colors as she slips into unconsciousness. The angels have come for her: her brothers and sisters, her mother still unsmiling, firm even in mercy. In these moments she can recall all of their faces in intimate detail, untouched by sickness: the soft curve of red cheeks and brown eyes rimmed by pale lashes. She can smell their skin and feel their breath all around her, the man and his grunts fading away to nothing. Such a disappointment it would be to wake in her body!

Clementine imagines her mother's face, wearing an expression almost like affection, the hint of a smile. She dreams of pressing her face to the chubby neck of her littlest brother, inhaling the baby scent of him. She forgets about her husband and their tiny room. Her mother, her brothers, her sisters her father, maybe, easy to imagine him dead—reaching for her. She can feel their hands, warm all around her. She slips from her skin like soap down a drain. Clementine neither harp nor drum nor girl, but a sliver of light in a boundless sky.

Fight

The man with the black mustache is almost too drunk to stand, almost too drunk to beat her. Almost. Clementine squats in a dark corner of the room, waiting for him, biding her time, her anger a glowing nugget of iron in her chest. She watches his lurching shadow on the far wall, lets him come close enough to the bed to raise his fist and pound the pillow where her head ought to lay.

Clementine's first swing with the hammer lands a glancing blow on the back of his shoulder. It is harder than she expected, harder than her husband led her to believe, to strike another person, to deliver a blow with intent. The hammer weighs heavy in her hand but she raises it again as he turns to face her. The whites of his eyes glow as the hammer arcs to meet his jaw.

She steps back as he spits out blood and bits of broken teeth. When she swings again, her husband's legs fail him and he collapses to the floor, making a wet whining noise through his nose. He weeps, his mustache tinged red. Clementine, teeth bared like a jackal, descends on the man and brings the hammer down again and again, until she grows tired, until the face with its black-red mustache is gone.

She changes into a clean dress and searches the man's pockets for money. Clementine sinks into a chair, weighing the coins and sweaty bills in her hand. It's enough. She sleeps for a time. Soon the sun will creep above the trees and burden the town with light, but for now the night is so dark and so still.

By Foot—turn to p. 11
By Train—turn to p. 13

By Foot

The road is deeply rutted and pock-marked by the hooves of horses and oxen, mud-slick in some places and dusty in others. She walks without hurry, brisk but careful, watching the path ahead of her and choosing her steps with care. She walks far enough that the sun sits high in its throne of clouds, far enough to sweat through the thin fabric of her dress, before the men catch up.

They say, *ma'am*, and she doesn't stop, *ma'am!*, and she ignores them. One man angles his horse ahead of her, forces her to stop and lift her head. Man and horse are dirty, stinking, their filth offensive. He scowls down at her and she wishes she had the strength to topple him and the horse together, send them both screaming to the ground. Somewhere behind her, another man dismounts, his saddle leather groaning. The devil inside her lifts its pointed head, hisses a warning.

The touch of a man's hand on her arm breaks her. Clementine whirls on him, digging for his eyes with her broken fingernails. The man screams and another man says, *Jesus*, his voice high and pinched like a woman's. Clementine squirms away, dodges around the horse, and runs. Her ankle twists against a hole in the road. She lets the pain spur her on. When a hand in her hair jerks her off her feet, she fights, kicking and biting and scratching like a cornered animal, overcome by blind instinct.

Let them take her to jail, lock her away forever. Let them throw a rope over a strong branch and hang her. The devil inside her foams at the mouth, eager, bloodthirsty, and Clementine has had enough of men. Let them feed her a bullet like a rabid dog. Let them come and put her down.

By Train

Clementine stops at the ticket window, her heart a tiny fluttering bird that beats against the cage of her chest. She waits to be recognized, to be marched away from the train station and handed over to the sheriff. A dark-haired man has the look of her husband and all the air goes out of her—but it's impossible, she's left him broken like mirror glass at the boarding house. The devil inside her sleeps coiled, unconcerned.

Ma'am, the man on the other side of the window says, rolling his eyes as though he is already bored of her. *St. Louis or San Francisco?*

Clementine cannot bear the thought of California. The place is poison in her mind. *St. Louis*, she says, sliding a mass of bills across the counter.

As the train lurches its way down the track, Clementine begins to relax, lets her shoulders rest against the faded seat cushion, worn flat by other journeys. In St. Louis, Clementine will decide where to go and how to live. She may go east as far as the coast or north to Chicago. She may live quietly as a widow. She may find work. She may find a man. She may let the devil decide. She doesn't know. She has time to plan, to plot.

She thinks of her father, that broken man, as she watches the sun paint the dusty prairie in shades of gold. She will check the papers for news of him, but she will not go to him. Her father, she thinks, will understand. He knows what it means to seek out a new path, to let your old life slip dark into the back of your memory. Clementine tips her face to the heat of an eager day. She will return to the light.

Escape

Clementine flees before the sun rises, stumbling down the narrow stairs, racing as if pursued. By dawn she slows, panting, her feet heavy and sore. She wishes for worn-in boots, lighter skirts, but does not stop to loosen her laces or sit a moment by the side of the road. *What if,* she thinks, *what if he is coming for me? What if he is just around the bend?* Fear makes her forget the twin aches of her feet.

As she walks, Clementine thinks of her father, their joyful reunion. She can see the route he traced on the map, curving north like a fat black serpent. They only have each other, now. She won't leave his side again, won't let herself be seduced by the promise of a lesser man. Clementine walks through the night, her path lit by the moon, awake yet dreaming of her father's voice. He calls out to her and she answers and feels less alone.

In the morning, a passing trader offers her a ride in his cart. Clementine eyes his dusty brown mule, a sack of bones and skin, but climbs in anyway. She knocks mud from her heels, settles in against bags of tobacco and salt. The world stands and Clementine passes.

The man takes her to the border. *California!* he says. His grin reveals black teeth like knobs of coal. The mule's four hooves have barely crossed when the man hauls him to a stop.

He says, *There's the matter of payment, for my services?*

He touches his cracked lips with the tip of his tongue. *You can make it up to me*, he says. *I know a way.*

Depart—turn to p. 17
Deal—turn to p. 19

Depart

In three days Clementine's legs fail her. She sits in the dirt for a moment, unable to remember how she came to be there, feet curled under her body. She rocks onto her hands and knees, tries to push upright even as her muscles shake, threatening collapse. Her breath comes in short panting gasps. She does not have tears to weep.

When she is calmer, Clementine begins to crawl. Her hands and knees scrape the baked earth. Unable to lift her body over ruts and muck in the road, she shoves through. She thinks, *Father.* Her dragging bones leave a wake like a plow. She thinks, *Gold.* Buttons pull free from her blouse and dust and tiny stones fill her dress, sharp against her pulled-tight skin. She thinks, *Water.* Still she crawls, reaching to claw at the road even as her fingers stain the dirt with blood.

Clementine sleeps and wakes hours later as the sun is setting. Orange light cast across the road before her reveals new tracks, two sturdy wagon wheels and hoof prints to match. Someone has passed without disturbing her, without pausing to help. Some man, she is sure.

Murderer, Clementine says through scabbed lips, *murderer murderer murderer.*

Around a bend she finds a deep hole and scoops out a handful of brown liquid. More sludge than puddle, more piss than water. Still Clementine does not hesitate to swallow. It slides foul and burning down her aching throat. She lowers her head to drink until the puddle is gone, then swallows handfuls of wet dirt. The mud and water sit high in her belly, won't go down. She rolls to the side of the road to retch under a bush and finds that she has neither the will nor the power to move again. The heavy night blankets her and she does not notice the chill in the air or the mess she has made of her clothes. She is already far from the road. She is only a tangle of bones, a handful of dust scattered by the wind.

Deal

Clementine stops washing. There's no way to rid her skin of the man's rotted smell, the agony of his touch. He comes to her at night when the fire rages. She watches their shadows on the ground, the humped shape of his body on hers. When he finishes, he kisses the side of her face. Sometimes he calls her by another woman's name. *You're a love, Sammy*, he says, or, *Thanks for the tussle, Annie*.

After the man rolls himself in his blanket, Clementine spreads his tattered map on the ground. He's promised to take her to San Francisco and from there, she hopes, she can follow her father's trail north. His claim is on a hill near the Feather River, in a wooded valley cradled against the bosom of a mountain. She knows that much. Clementine studies the map for some clue to its location. How big a hill? How long a journey?

They come to San Francisco tired and stinking, Clementine walking with one hand on the wagon, letting it hold her up. Mud sucks at her feet, strokes her calves with wet fingers. Her lungs burn with the effort. When they stop at the side of the road, Clementine and the mule bend to the trough, the water cool and cloudy. As she rinses sweat from her eyes, she catches a glimpse of the man disappearing through the swinging doors of a lopsided hotel. *Good riddance*, she thinks, but loneliness settles on her.

Clementine follows and turns back, and follows again. She knows his business by the look of the women draped over the porch railing. They wear dresses cinched around the waist and falling off their shoulders. One blows a kiss to Clementine, leans over the rail as though she is reaching for an embrace.

The whore calls: *You need work, baby? Gotta home for you here.* Clementine shudders as the women laugh, a noise dry and hollow as rattling bones.

San Francisco—turn to p. 21
The Hills—turn to p. 23

San Francisco

Clementine takes a job in a low-rent hotel, assured by the madam that there will be no trouble from the men. With such a glut of easy sex, they don't notice her. She cooks and cleans, stirs boiling laundry in a huge black cauldron. She keeps her head down, keeps to herself. The swish of a broom over a wood floor offers a kind of comfort, a soothing ordinary task. For a while the girls take to calling her Cherry, but soon they forget, move on to another sport. Clementine gets along.

There is a quiet hour in the late morning that Clementine regards as her own. The girls take to their beds with full bellies and drooping eyes and the man behind the bar shutters the windows. Clementine uses this hour to slip outside with a mug of weak coffee and stand on the sagging porch. She looks down the wide road, watches as men and horses churn the mud anew. The thought of leaving, of fighting through the sucking mud, exhausts her.

Clementine thinks of her father and his little wagon stacked with the food and supplies. Months ago they left the empty corpse of the farm and headed west, hopeful. She can hardly remember the farm now, or her mother's face. She remembers dusty winds and crackling dry heat, a baby crying, the stink of sweat and fever. Some other Clementine walked for weeks beside the wagon and thanked God for the loss of her mother and her brothers and sisters, glad of any reason to leave. Some other Clementine married a stranger, abandoned him in the night.

Her father may yet pass through town. The law may yet come searching for her. They may see her and look through her and move on. She's gone shy, gone modest. She washes dishes and scrubs on her knees, hair braided tight. For Clementine each sun rises no better or worse than the one before. She tucks hope and happiness away in her bottom drawer.

Even if they stopped to stare, Clementine is sure no one would recognize her old self. That life is over. That girl is dead.

The Hills

Clementine crosses a river, a mountain, another river, so many hills that she doesn't have the numbers to count them all. She walks and walks and wonders if she is gaining any ground. Somewhere ahead a river rages. She can smell the froth in the air. She stops to lean against a tree and there he is, climbing the hill towards her like something out of a dream.

Papa, she says. He stops, bent almost in half under the weight of pack and pick and pan. They stand, staring. Clementine waits for him to throw down his load and open his arms to her. All that she has endured on this long, terrible slog seems suddenly worth the price of her pride and hope and body. Here is one man, at last, she can depend on.

Clementine, he says. His whole face trembles.

I came back, she says. She takes two steps toward him. Her father shudders, shaking as though he is a helpless fawn and she a prowling coyote. *I left him*, she says. *I ran away. I escaped.* She reaches to take his hand and he flinches.

He sighs, blowing hard through his nose. *No, you should not have come.*

Papa, I'm here now, she says, reaching for him. He dodges her touch with the agility of a cat. She cries and he stands and watches her. *Father!*

He shrugs against the straps of his pack, adjusting the weight. He cuts one last look at her and then advances up the narrow trail. Clementine grips his arm, tries to make him stop, and he shakes her off like so much dust. He leaves her as easily as he would drop a worn shoe or the bones of his dinner, picked clean and broken.

Later Clementine cannot remember choosing a rock from the many scattered about the trees, only the pleasant weight of it in her hand. She cannot remember her father falling, though he must have—he lays there still. She plunges her arms into the cold water of a fast stream and recalls a harsh cry, like a bird in distress, from somewhere far away. She scrubs her hands until they are white and shining through the water, and then she sits back to admire her work.

The Gold Claim

Every day, from the first glint of dawn to the barest scrap of light at sundown, they work the claim. Her father digs and Clementine pans, sloshing the water just so against the sides of the shallow bowl. She builds dams and hammers rock. She works to the refrain of her father's promises: *Soon, soon, soon...*

Clementine's hands blister and split. She aches. The thrill of leaving the farm, the promise of a new life—thinking back on her ignorance makes Clementine want to spit, to tear out her hair in a fit of anger. Mining and farming aren't so different, it's the same toil and the same muck, the same unending work for even less reward. She walked a thousand miles west to live the same life in new scenery.

Now and then her father's pans come out of the creek sparkling. Gold so fine it's hardly more than dust, but any gold is reason enough to stay. In her wretched moments, Clementine imagines pouring all the gold into her hand and puffing up her cheeks and scattering all their fortune to the winds. Their fortune! They've collected so little that the ruts in her palms would barely be lined. Hardly worth the breath of air she would need to blow it away.

At night—chewing a mouthful of solid-dried meat, tasting of dust and misery—Clementine's anger rears up from her gut like a winged thing. She imagines screaming at her father, striking him, demanding that they leave. He is so frail, so gaunt, she could overpower him. With her mother gone, Clementine must be their strength. She sees her father as her mother must have: small and weak, a flimsy excuse for a man.

But she stays. She could have found a home anywhere along the way and did not. Saw opportunities and did not act on them, too afraid to leave him. Sure that one or the other would die if they were separated. Afraid it might be him. Afraid it might not be. She does not want to imagine her bones confined to this ground, her soul wandering uneasy for eternity.

Clementine sits on her anger. It is her fault as much as his that they have come to this place. Her father tries, in his own way. When her boots wear out and her feet leave bloody smears on the rocks, he brings her two old herring boxes. A poor substitute, a sad joke, but Clementine has little hope for a better option.

Herring Boxes—turn to p. 27
Bare Feet—turn to p. 37

Herring Boxes

She stuffs the boxes with rags and tears filthy strips from the hem of her dress to tie them to her feet. Still they flop or chafe or catch on tree roots and send her sprawling, and the stink is constant. Clementine must periodically slide them off her feet and dig long slivers of wood from her flesh. Blood spots the rags like tiny blossoms, stark red before layers of dirt and grime and fresh blood from new wounds coat them. She stays close to the small lean-to that has become their home, fears seeing anyone if she strays too far. Does not want to broadcast her shame.

Clementine spends her days in dreams. As she makes a stew of small, bony fish, she thinks of the warm copper smell of blood, of butchered hogs and sizzling fat. As she collects firewood, she remembers new leather boots, supple and soft. As she sits by the stream swishing dirt in the pan, she longs for a proper house, a roof, walls, a table, chairs. Clementine craves and she wants and she hungers. In this way, time passes.

If her father has desires, he doesn't speak of them to her. Each morning he holds the glass vial of gold dust in his thin fist and tips it from one side to the other, watching the tiny grains float. He says, *Clem honey, we are being tested We must persevere.* Sometimes

Clementine can see the ghost of her mother beside him, lips curled into a snarl.

Even the dead mock us, she thinks. *We are being tested. We are found wanting.*

In the cold emptiness of night, her father is less inclined to preach patience. She sees the exhaustion in him, back swayed like a plow horse due for the bullet.

We could leave, Clementine says. *Pack up and go home. Find some other way to kill ourselves.*

Her father stares at her from across the fire. His thin body shakes. He says, in a voice barely more than a whisper, *Is that what you want?*

Retreat—turn to p. 29
Remain—turn to p. 31

Retreat

In San Francisco the air is sweet with promises. It wraps itself around Clementine and weaves in and out of her hair like ribbons. Here are people who smile and laugh, who have left the dirty mining camps behind or never set foot in them. She doesn't mind that she is barefoot, that her long hair is matted and tangled. They are leaving. They are on the road to gone.

Clementine sells their old tools and supplies, useless now, while her father sits outside a boarding house and lets the mud soak into his pants. She shows him a fistful of paper and coins and he nods without looking. His eyes go right through her, staring back the way they've come, towards the mountain and the sick, miserly claim. He won't let her sell the gold, but she makes enough for two tickets on the next day's train. They'll go east, resettle somewhere past the choking desert. A town, Clementine promises herself, not a farm. She gets them a room at the boarding house and spends her last coin on a pair of blue slippers, appealing because they are so unsuited for hard living, so wrong for a miner's daughter. Is she a miner's daughter? No, not anymore.

In their room, her father sits on the bed, won't listen to her when she clucks at him not to dirty the linens. He stares at the floorboards while Clementine flits around him. She can't keep still. There is too much to see and to touch, bustling streets and a chipped porcelain ewer. When was the last time she held something so lovely? She will have only lovely things now.

Clementine chirps and hums, skips about the small room. Her father will not acknowledge her joy, will not speak to her. He will not speak to her all that night and he will not speak to her when they board the train. He will not speak and Clementine will not wonder, not until they are past the desert and chugging through the scrubby plains, what it is that makes him cover his face with his hands. Clementine, drunk on the joy of leaving, will not stop to consider what it is he has left behind.

Remain

Clementine sees him for the first time as she wades into a shallow stream, letting the water soothe her torn-up feet. She catches a glimpse of him through the trees, squatting half underneath a clump of bushes. At first she misunderstands, thinks he's relieving himself, but then he swings his ax down hard and she realizes he's caught something in a snare. A rabbit. Her mouth fills with saliva, she can almost feel the meat sliding down her throat. The man stands with his prize and even from a distance she sees him grin.

She watches him walk closer, but is surprised to find him suddenly standing near. She smells his sweat and the rabbit blood, feels the heat coming off his skin. He is young but not a boy, his face tanned and his eyes shining. Clementine wants to feel the roughness of his beard against her face. She blushes at the thought.

She takes the man back to meet her father, cleans and skins the rabbit while they talk about gold and mines and rock. The young man hasn't found any gold yet, but he doesn't seem to mind. He is all light and breezes, smiles and laughter. He talks about heading north, to Yukon Territory, where weaker men are afraid to mine. He has plans. Clementine eats a share of the rabbit, but it is the man that settles in her stomach, winds around her like a second skin.

The young man stays until night falls and then stands, bouncing on the balls of his feet. Clementine's father shakes his hand, thanks him for the rabbit, wishes him well. The man turns to Clementine, lips curling around her name. He touches her wrist. Clementine feels a surge of something like hunger course through her, hard and sudden as a slap. Firelight reflects in the man's eyes. She feels the heat coming off him.

A Marriage—turn to p. 33
A Maid—turn to p. 35

A Marriage

Her husband's claim reveals its treasures. At first, like her father, he found only dust and flakes. Then he struck the right rock and found a vein yellow and glistening like a cracked egg. He skipped down to the camp and lifted Clementine off her feet, whooping. She cried when he pressed a gold-striped hunk of stone in her hand.

Still he talks about the Yukon. In the darkness of their bed he talks of nuggets the size of a man's fist as though seducing her. Entering her, he says, *As thick on the ground as these pines.* Sweat-slick and thrusting, he says, *Waiting to be found by any man brave enough to go look—ah, Clem!* Clementine indulges his fantasy, but she remembers the promises made to her father about easy riches and the disappointment of finding his claim dry as a nun. Success makes dreams come easy, makes men forget how it was. How it could always be again.

When her husband sleeps beside her, Clementine listens to his breathing, strains for any sounds beyond the tent walls. The heavy canvas blocks the wind and the chirps and rustles that she has grown accustomed to hearing. At first she was excited by the sleeping pallet and its bed of old furs, the lop-sided table, the hanging lantern that could keep the tent as bright as any morning. Now she finds she misses the stars overhead, the creaking of pine boughs. Though she has never given a thought to shutting doors, when the tent flap falls closed it seems final, inescapable.

She thinks of her father in his lean-to, his vial of dust. Her husband took her from that life and gave her another and she is glad of it. Someday they will grow rich. She will have a house with glass windows, a settled life, and only vague memories of a farm and a mine. Until then she is a miner's wife, the pick and ax her children. Until then she clings to the side of a hill, prays for good fortune and hopes that she has not made a terrible mistake.

A Maid

Married to the mountain, Pa is fond of saying. The mountain heaves and shrugs one morning like a brawler flexing his muscles, sending miners fleeing to the lowlands, a trail of discarded tools in their wake. Clementine isn't surprised when Pa stops his panning and turns to her, his face aglow with gold lust even as the hum of the earthshake hangs in the air. He says, *Let's visit our wife. She'll be lonesome.*

Inside the long tunnel, Clementine trots to keep up, not wanting to be left in darkness. She dares not look over her shoulder, cannot bear to see the bright spot of blue sky grow smaller. She focuses on the winking lantern flame, her father's white hair, his stooped back. He is her tether, keeps her from being swallowed by shadows.

Her father chooses a spot, hangs the lantern on a nail. A pebble skips past, moving of its own will. *How funny*, Clementine thinks, even as the soft hairs on her arms stand on end. She puts one hand on the rock as he swings the pick, feels the vibration all the way up her arm and into her spine. They all share the same heartbeat: Clementine, her father, the mountain. She sighs and the mountain seems to sigh as well. We should leave, she wants to say, but can't speak. Danger hangs in the air, choking her.

When he steps back to wipe his face, he points to a thin stripe, delicate as a fish bone. Gold? Does it shine? Hard to tell in the dim light of the tunnel, everything so dusty and jagged. She traces the streak and feels a tremor go through the wall as the mountain wakes. Her father's hand closes around her arm and the lantern falls, goes out. He pulls her, shoves her, but in the darkness she doesn't know which way he means her to turn. Their wife roars and then there is no sound but rending, tearing, battering rock, and then she does not hear anything.

Bare Feet

Clementine's feet harden. Soon she can skip over the rocks, up and down the hills, easy as a goat. The sun tans her skin honey brown, fades her glowing yellow hair to the color of light on mist. She remembers what it was like to live in a house, but she misses it less. She doesn't concern herself with those memories.

Over and over Clementine patches her last dress, her father's tattered canvas bags. She sews for miners who have left their wives behind or had no wives to leave. She coaxes unraveled threads back into line and reinforces thin knees, thin elbows, thinner spirits. She learns their names. She earns a reputation. The miners shuffle onto her father's claim, nod and mumble and pay her in gold dust or fresh meat or old fabric. She takes half a ragged quilt in trade and for a time patches holes with scraps of dainty flowers, blooming pink against the dirt and sweat of camp.

She has a place. If Clementine does not grow to love the mining life, she at least finds herself feeling a thing like happiness. She tries not to think hard on this feeling, does not want to crush it in her over-eager hands. She builds it inside herself like a nest, piece by fragile piece. If she works at it long enough and stays very quiet, something may squat down and settle there.

One sun-dappled evening, a miner brings four speckled geese to the claim, wriggling feathered bodies tucked under his arms. They honk and struggle against him, long necks thrashing. Clementine is almost seduced by the promise of meat, of eggs, of goslings. Four geese could sustain them a while. *What else?* she asks. She doesn't want to look eager. She has the upper hand.

I have soap, the miner says. His shirt is torn, gaping open like a broken heart. He needs her.

Clementine can hardly believe her good fortune. That either should be offered on that lonely hilltop, that she could access such treasures, sends a burst of warmth up her spine. She twists her hands in her skirt and curls her toes into the packed dirt beneath her feet. She tries not to grin.

Geese—turn to p. 39
Soap—turn to p. 45

Geese

While Clementine sews, the man fashions a little hut for the geese out of scrap wood and branches. *They like to sleep inside,* he tells her as he leaves. He watches the birds over her shoulder, his eyes misting, as though he is leaving his children in her care. Clementine pushes her pity aside. Her loneliness is just as big as his. She hasn't taken what he wasn't willing to offer.

She sits up half the night, listening for any sound of distress from the geese's hut, but they are silent. In the morning they waddle into the sunlight, stretching their necks and their big brown wings. They're more or less like big chickens, stupid and slow as any farm bird. Now and then one of them regards her from the depths of a beady black eye, but mostly they poke about in the dirt and grass, make soft shushing noises to one another. She wonders if geese are capable of sighing or if she's imagined the tone of wistfulness in their chatter.

Clementine has chores of her own, no choice but to let the birds wander. Still she looks for them as she gathers wood, keeps them in her sight. She carries her father's heavy bag to the claim and races back to camp, to her geese, counts the silver-brown backs over and over, to be sure none of the four has slipped away or met a fox or a hungry miner. She stops often just to watch them, to spend a quiet moment enjoying the ownership of such a hearty, graceful flock.

When her father returns for his midday meal, he catches her sitting dumb by the fire and she rushes to finish the cooking. He nudges her out of the way, takes the skillet out of her hand and settles himself with a grunt.

He says, *Have you seen them on the water?*

When Clementine shakes her head, he smiles. *You should.*

Geese to Water—turn to p. 41
Water to Geese—turn to p. 43

Geese to Water

Clementine says, *All right, geese*. She claps her hands. *Move it*. Two
of the geese raise their heads from the dry grass, blink at her. She
clucks at them, claps again. They waddle a few steps before stopping
to graze. One spreads its great wings and flaps, showing off a breast
the color of old snow, plump and round.

Clementine herds the geese in a meandering serpentine down
the little meadow towards the river. She swishes her skirts at them,
as though she is a great bird, and they shake their tails. They hiss
and she replies in their own language through gritted teeth. By the
time she hears the water tumbling downstream, Clementine's dress
is damp with sweat and her hair dangles loose and heavy from her
braid.

The geese hear the water too. They waddle to the river's edge to
drink and splash in the shallows. Clementine watches the water
bead on their feathers, dribble from their beaks and down the long
slopes of their necks. They seem happy in the water—and why not,
with the sun hot overhead and no shade to rest under? She strips
off her dress and wades into the river in her underthings, the water
cold as a grave.

She walks deeper and deeper across the slick rocks, gripping with
her toes, until the riverbed gives way to a trench. Clementine loses

her footing and can't find it again, thrashes and kicks and struggles to keep her head above the water. She tries to scream for help but her mouth fills with water. For a tiny moment she catches sight of the geese near the shore, watching her with their empty black eyes, unblinking.

She sees the milky yellow sun above her and bubbles all around her. She sees water and glittering starbursts at the edges of her vision. She sees water and her ghost-white hands, feels her chest about to burst and her underskirt wrapped around her ankles. She sees water and then she sees nothing, her sightless eyes no use to her now, her limbs forgetting to claw and kick, the water and only the water, down and down and down.

Water to Geese

Her father's tin pan is a good shape, roughly goose-sized. Clementine fills it with cool water from the river and sets it out for them. She sits with her father in the shade, watching the geese splash and preen. Drops of water on their feathers catch the afternoon sun and shine like fool's gold. Twice they tip the pan, two geese trying to squeeze in at once and failing in a flurry of flapping and wild honks. Her father laughs, puts one hand on her shoulder. A thought comes to Clementine unbidden: *We are happy.*

She waits for the claim to give birth to their fortune and in the meantime Clementine loses herself to the pleasure of planning. Soon they will have eggs, more than enough. While her father mines, Clementine can barter and trade. The cramped lean-to made of sticks may become a sturdy wall, and then two walls, and then three with a canvas roof. Clementine imagines a miner's wife, new to camp and heartsick and hungry, trading a pair of boots for a basket of eggs. She will admire the shape of her feet in the soft leather, the ease of moving along a rocky path. What a luxury to have tender feet, to not worry.

Clementine will raise goslings, a squawking brood that grows fast into smoked meat and down pillows. A few smart trades and the canvas roof could be replaced with woven branches, a thick grass thatch. They will sleep warm and dry in their little room.

For Christmas, a whole goose, every miner's plate heaped with roasted flesh. Dreams follow dreams: shingles, a pot-bellied stove in the corner, planks on the floor, smooth and polished. A town may grow from camp, men coming with their horses and silver spurs and new goods to trade. Roads and shops and neat rows of houses. Hope comes easy with a full belly. Clementine at last is fit to burst.

Soap

Clementine wraps the precious nub of soap in an old handkerchief, buries it in a corner of the lean-to, near her sleeping pallet. She wants to wait until the end of the day or the first rays of morning, some time when she can be alone and bathe at leisure. But the brown flashes of her dirt-caked fingers seem more heinous than usual. She can feel the dried sweat under her arms and down the center of her back. Her scalp itches.

She drops the kindling she has been gathering, certain that ants and spiders are creeping over her skin, and claws the packet of soap out of the ground. Clementine means to walk, but finds herself running to the river's edge. Seams rip as she pulls off her clothes, but no matter. Later she can sew everything back together, later when she is clean.

Clementine plunges into the cold water, falls to her knees in the shallows. With handfuls of sand and grit, she scrubs layers of dirt and sweat and grime from her limbs, already prickling with goose-flesh. She works the soap into a hearty lather, washes it downriver and lathers again, over and over until her skin shines pink and clean. She washes all of her parts in the bright afternoon sun, lifting her breasts and spreading her thighs. She untangles her hair with soap-slick fingers, picks out the knots and matted hunks. Slowly, slowly, a girl emerges.

At last, shivering but clean, Clementine wades deeper into the river and lets the water rush over her. She braces herself on a cluster of rocks and admires the white gleam of her stomach through the water, like fine china. As she twists her hair over one shoulder, Clementine notices a figure on shore. The man who traded sewing for soap stands with one boot in the center of the pile of her discarded clothes. Clementine draws her knees to her chest, crouches as low as she can get, but he's seen her. He crooks a finger, beckoning. The slow spread of his smile settles frosty on her skin. Rising from the water, she smells the stink of her fear.

Confront—turn to p. 47
Cower—turn to p. 49

Confront

Clementine curses herself as a fool, a harlot. Bathing in the middle of the day, naked as her wedding night—can she be surprised that someone saw? Did she expect to go unnoticed, unpunished for her wanton display? She hears her mother's voice, clear and strong as if the woman was still alive. *No less than any slut deserves.*

The man takes a step towards her, water splashing over his big boots, his solid legs. He will come for her, stupid girl trapped by the river, too wide, too deep. She stands, pulls her hair forward over her shoulders, tries to hide as much as she can from the man's steady gaze. She looks past the man, through him, scanning the tree line. The meadow is empty. Even the wind has gone. She will have to trust that she is fast enough to get away. There is no one to call for help. She spins, lunges, runs for shore.

Too slow. The man grabs her by the hair, winding it around his fist. Clementine tries to dodge around him. Let him rip her head bald, let him take that as his prize. He grabs her wrist, pulls her close against him. She winces at his grip on her hair, struggles as he forces her to look up at him. His lips are chapped and cracked, bloody at the corners. He lowers his face to the curve of her neck and she feels the musty heat of his mouth. In quick, panting breaths like a dog, he sniffs her.

A sound wells up inside Clementine and escapes before she can grit her teeth against it, a squeal like a rabbit in a snare. The man laughs when she tries to claw his face. He bites her shoulder, the grip of his mouth jagged and uneven where his teeth are broken or missing. A muddy layer of grit forms between them as his clothing rubs her wet skin. All around her is the filth of the man, filling her nostrils. Touching her. Clementine screams but there is no one to hear. She prays it will be over soon.

Cower

Clementine kneels under the water until everything below her lips is submerged. She watches the man for any sign that he is leaving or coming after her. Would he follow her into the water? She's close enough to shore that he wouldn't have to swim, big enough that he wouldn't have to fight hard against the current. If he wants her bad enough, he'll come. There's nowhere for her to go but deeper.

I'll wait, the man says. *Wait right here for you to finish your business.* He laughs like wood splitting.

She can feel the tug of the river's flow all around her. She could try to reach the other bank, but it's stronger in the middle, deeper, with hidden trenches and whirlpools. Better to wait him out. To bide her time. Clementine shivers, sending out little ripples in every direction. She rubs her arms, slaps at her legs, bites down hard on her lips to still her chattering teeth.

I'm not picky, the man says. *You look clean enough for me, darlin'.*

As Clementine watches the man and the man watches Clementine, the sun slides toward the tree line. The tall narrow trees throw long shadows across the meadow. They remind her of plow furrows, of a field waiting to be planted. She remembers the farm, the smell of dirt after rain, the air rich and heavy. She is heavy, a heavy girl-tree growing roots in a river. Her teeth click against each other like coins in a purse. She can't stop shaking.

Goddammit, girl, the man says. He charges into the river, reaching for her.

Clementine thinks, *Get away.* She jerks and loses her place among the rocks. The current sweeps her legs out from under her. Water rushes over her face, but she is too tired to fight. Let the current have its way. The river seems to have come alive, as though a thousand pairs of hands hold her, pass her downstream. Warmth blooms the length of her cold bones. The river cradles her like a lover. The river takes her home.

Cate O'Toole was awarded a Rachel Carson Fellowship and earned her MFA in fiction from Chatham University. She is the author of the chapbook *Big Women, Big Girls* (Stamped Books, 2011) and her stories have appeared in *Six Sentences* and the *6S Vol. 1* anthology, *Wanderlust Review, the Linnet's Wings, shady side review* and elsewhere. Cate was the 2012 recipient of the Poetry & Prose Winter Getaway's Jan-Ai Scholarship. She lives and writes in Seattle, WA. You can find Cate online at lifeaftermfa.wordpress.com.